Santa Claus
is on a
DIET!

written by
NANCY SCOTT-CAMERON

illustrated by
CRAIG CONLAN

This Christmas story
is for all little children,
especially Adam and Christopher

Nancy Scott-Cameron

For B.H.
who kept me feeling
Christmassy all summer long

Craig Conlan

Text copyright ©2006 Nancy Scott Cameron. Edited by Mogzilla.
Illustrations copyright ©2006 Craig Conlan.

Cover design by Craig Conlan. Edited by Mogzilla. Pre-press by Surface Impression.

First published by Mogzilla in 2007.

5 4 3 2 1

ISBN 10: 09546576-9-1
ISBN 13: 978-0-9546576-9-7

Printed in Malta.

Mrs. Claus looked Santa up and down.
She shook her head - began to frown.

Santa dearest, the problem's that,
in plain words, darling...

Santa said,
"I guess you're right,
This old red suit
does feel too tight.

I must lose weight,
protect my heart.
I'll see the doctor,
for a start."

So off they went to **Dr. Brown**
who said, "**PLease** come and sit right down.
Thank goodness, yes, your heart's **OK**.
We **must** make sure it **stays** that way."

"Change your diet and you'll see,
how much fitter you will be.
Eat lots of veg like sprouts and peas.
Cut down on butter, eggs and cheese."

"Instead of **cake** have **grapes** or **cherries**. Or a **healthy shake** with **berries**."

The reindeer, hearing of his plan,
    said, "We'll **help** Santa all we can."

"Last year he was so **overweight**.
    We huffed and puffed and turned up **late!**"

All the **elves** were helpful too.
"**We'll** eat all your **sweets** for you!"

Santa took his weekly hike!

And bought himself a brand new bike!

At the gym he worked and worked!

They all made sure he never shirked.

Many months of sticking to it...
Santa thought he'd never do it...
Four sizes smaller- looking trim.
Proud that there was less of him.

His Santa suit was **far too wide.**
He could almost **turn** around inside.
Slim beyond his **wildest dreams!**
Mrs Claus took **in** the **seams.**

On the launch pad, all was solemn.
"Mrs. Claus - we have a problem!"

Looking at each deer he said
"You just aren't fit to pull my sled!"

Next Christmas...

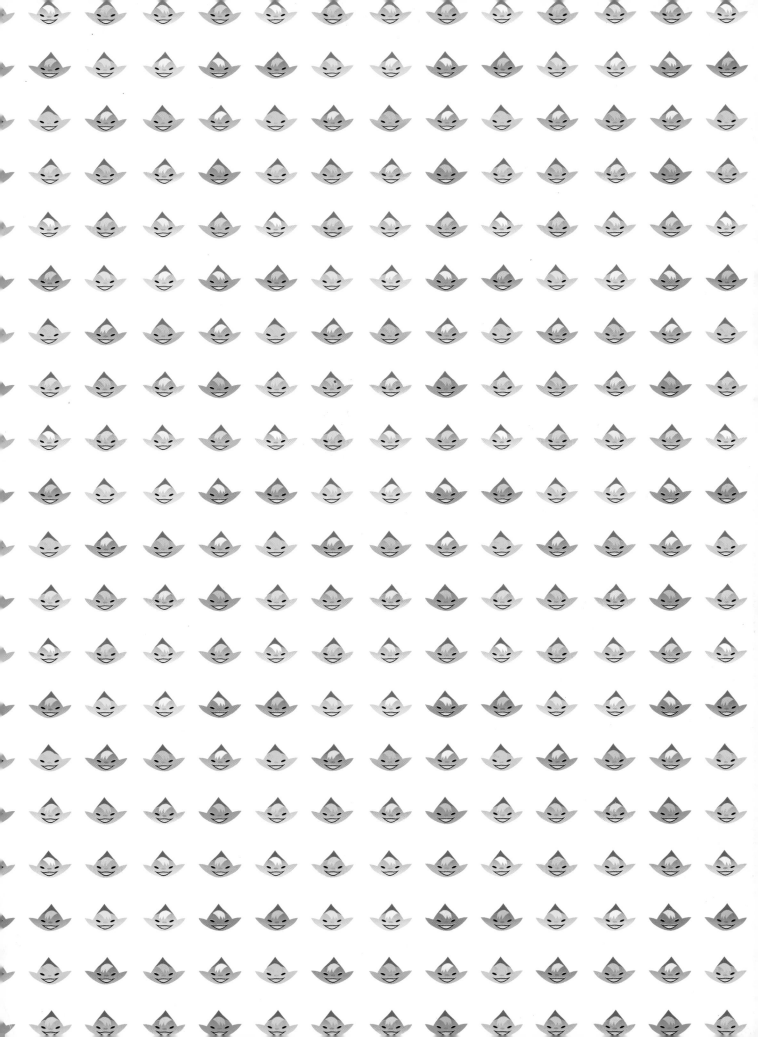

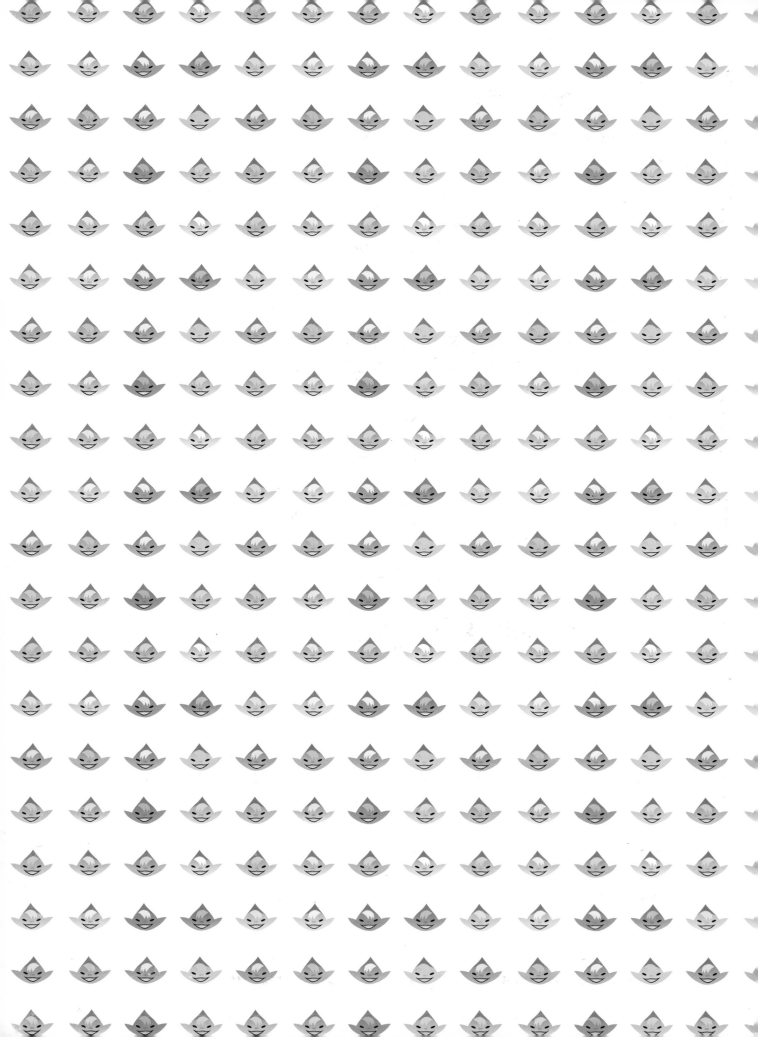